A BAR IN PARIS

IMOGENE NIX

Print ISBN 9780995418295

*Written many years ago, this is the first time A Bar
In Paris has made it into print.
I'm immensely proud of this story, because it broke
my personal writing barriers allowing me to explore
something many women fantasize about... Freedom
to pursue their own sexual needs.
In doing so, I have to thank my husband who read
this story and offered his suggestions. To my family
who understand the closed office door means I'm
writing a naughty scene and to my readers.*

Imogene

2019

BLURB

Turning 30? All alone? A commitment-free weekend in Paris should help...shouldn't it?

What does a single woman do when she's turning thirty? She takes a weekend trip to Paris looking for commitment-free sex. Or that's what Davina Chandler does, anyway.

Enter Johnathon, a tall, charming Englishman. How can she possibly resist his magnetism and that sexy dimple?

What starts out as a lark quickly becomes so much more, but can one weekend turn into a lifetime? And will a lie of omission bring everything into jeopardy?

CHAPTER ONE

The little pub on a street corner of Paris had been slowly emptying in the last hour, but I nursed my latest wine, checking out the thinning crowd. I'd been taking an occasional sip until the glass was empty before hailing the bartender to refill it. *"Excusez-moi?"* Once a fresh glass was in hand, I began my hunt again.

Yesterday, I'd flown in from London, where I work for a finance company on loan. My plan was simple. I needed to find a sexy guy to pass the entire weekend with. I intended to work off my current frustrations, both social and sexual, with this nameless, faceless man. I planned on it being both hot and commitment-free. Sex was on offer, and I planned to enjoy it.

The lack of sex was one of the drawbacks to my single status. When I was frustrated, the only guy to turn to was BOB—my battery operated boyfriend. And it seemed a bit cold and lonely sometimes. Every now and again I yearned for flesh on flesh, but there wasn't even a convenient lover hanging around in the wings.

So the trip to Paris was a gift from me to myself. It

seemed somehow appropriate, given that at the age of thirty, I was alone and desperately in need. "Happy birthday, me."

Over the last few years, all my friends had paired off. Some had married and some now had children. I'd worked hard, focusing on my career since taking the transfer to London. I had climbed the corporate ladder and proudly told my bosses I was married to the job. But at two in the morning, when I hungered after a particularly rocking dream...well, reaching for the bedside drawer left something to be desired. "At least I didn't have to pay for his plane ticket."

It might be the weekend of my thirtieth birthday, and I might have come in here to get lucky, but with the choices as slim as they were...well, I wasn't sure this was the right place to hang out. So far, there had been lots of sloppy, drunken Englishmen, a few Italians, and the odd Frenchman. None of the men I'd scanned had been either single or young, which had been part of my pick-a-man criteria. I seriously doubted they'd be able to manage anything interesting in bed. I toyed with the coaster on the polished table in front of me.

Maybe it was time to head back to my hotel across the way. I had set aside four days to howl. There was still plenty of time, I told myself, with a knee jigging up and down, staving off the hunger deep inside me.

I drained my glass of full-bodied red wine, feeling rather ambivalent about the whole situation. The waiter caught my eye and brought me a top up. "*Merci.*"

Might as well drink it before I left. He took the Euros I extended with a smile and a nod, his eyes darting to and fro. For a moment, I wondered if he knew why I was there, then mentally laughed at myself. He couldn't possibly know, of course.

I propped my elbows on the wood table and looked around. The bar was emptier than earlier in the night, which meant I could scan the room more easily. It was an older, renovated space, all wood and dark colors, with fake gaslight lanterns. They certainly added to the ambience. The chairs were covered in deep red velvet and the tabletops glistened in the light. Above the counter, hanging down, were sparkling glasses which reflected the brass fittings.

The waiter smiled and I sighed. "Time to go." As I prepared to rise, gripping my bag in my hand, the bell above the door rang and I watched with interest as the sexiest man I'd ever seen entered. The cool blonde on his arm was scowling and he pried her fingers from his arm then walked away. For a moment, she wobbled on her stilettos before she sneered in her super chic French way only they can pull off and stalked out the door. It slammed so hard the panes of glass shuddered.

The man scowled, but to be honest, it didn't hurt at all. He was tall and well built. Blond hair with gray eyes.

My mind screamed that this man could probably satisfy my needs. He didn't appear even slightly inebriated and he was obviously single now, if that little carry-on was to go by. Perhaps this was my chance? I smoothed down my black dress, making sure my cleavage was just peeking out, then I sucked in a deep, deep breath and stood, hoping to catch his eye.

I watched the man stalk to the bar and order in perfect English-accented French. *"Une bière, s'il vous plait."*

My toes curled at his voice and the waiter hurried to do his bidding. Mr. Sexy's voice was cultured and deep. I like voices, particularly men's voices. They can make me go gooey at the knees, and this one warmed my insides to the consistency of thick, warm honey. And I knew he was the one I wanted to be with all night long.

The server handed over a bottle of beer and a glass, but Mr. Sexy looked at the bottle, grimaced, and then took a long pull.

The other men at the bar started talking in low voices, putting aside newspapers. They paid their money and left. I didn't want to think it was because of the dangerous aura surrounding the man. It was, after all, three in the morning. No, there had to be something else. But I was sure it wasn't the time to ask these questions.

The small bar was quiet now as I was waiting alone with the mystery man. The waiter disappeared to the back. Obviously, with only two patrons left, he could do other things.

I sucked in my confidence, folded it around me like a coat, and approached the man. "Hi. Mind if I join you?"

He grinned and gestured to the seat beside him. I slipped onto the small stool, perched uncertainly. Then I wiggled my bum a little, thrust out my chest, and gave him my very best come-on smile.

"Looking for a hook up, are you?" His voice caused a curl of heat to gather deep inside me.

I nodded slowly. Better to be honest from the start, I thought. I didn't have time to say a word. The next thing I knew, he had me thrust against the bar, his lips on mine and his tongue halfway down my throat. But man, what a tongue it was.

He played me like a violin until he lifted his head, casting a wicked smile in my direction. "Your hotel or mine?"

"Umm, yours." Right now, I felt the rosy glow of arousal

roaring through me. Sexy and quick to catch on. Yep, I was sure this guy was a winner.

"You're not from around here, are you?"

I shook my head. "No."

Oh God! I'd never done this before and wasn't certain if I should ask for a name. I wasn't sure if I should ask if he had a handy condom. None of these things had been covered by the magazine article that suggested a quickie weekend tryst was the way to satisfy a single, thirties woman about town who was desperately horny.

As he drew away, I was hot and heady and he slipped his hand into mine.

"*Serveur? Que dois-je?*" He checked his small tab and the waiter hurried back, naming a price. It was all very quick and the waiter frowned a bit, seeing that I had changed spots and was obviously leaving with this man.

Then together, we rose and left the bar.

I STEPPED INSIDE HIS LUSH ROOM AT THE SAME HOTEL I was staying at. I'd booked a nice double with a balcony and sitting area. His room was obviously a suite, with a sitting area separate from the bed, and decorated in a bright pink. Garish, yes, but certainly unforgettable.

I slipped my shoes off as we entered, feeling the plush carpeting swallow them, and padded across the room. Paris by night is a wonderful sight to behold, I thought. The twinkling lights that never seem to go out called to me and I had to go to the window to chance a look. I sighed, accepting that Paris has an air unfound anywhere else. One that tells us it's been here for centuries and will remain long after we have passed.

I laughed a little at those whimsical thoughts. "It's amazing." Here I was, an Aussie in Paris, taking a break from the hubbub of London just long enough to have a sexy weekend interlude with a stranger was almost giggle-worthy. Because turning thirty meant respectability knocked, and this was the most disrespectable thing I'd ever done. Yep, perhaps I'd lost my marbles after all.

The man, whose name I didn't even know, cleared his throat. "Would you like a glass of champagne?"

"Sure." I nodded, thinking that there must be a way I could draw this out before committing to the act. Suddenly, what had seemed like a damn good idea sitting in my office on a damp and dreary May morning had overtones of 'Oh my God, it's really happening'. I was here. In a hotel room. With a stranger. In Paris. Planning on having sex. Just because I needed it.

He smiled, and once more I swallowed at the sight of the most amazingly sexy man I had ever seen. Truly, with sandy colored hair and gray-blue eyes that crinkled at the edges, how could I possibly go wrong?

My insides quivered as he walked to the phone and picked up the receiver, looking at me intently as if he knew the internal struggle happening in my mind. He punched a button. "*Service de chambre? J'aimerais commander une bouteille de champagne. Peut-être un Veuve Clicquot?*"

Now my French is pretty good, it has to be in my job, but the order for a bottle of Veuve Clicquot just rolled off his tongue like a native. A thread of interest wove around me as I watched him dispense with his tie, throwing it on the seat beside him.

He looked at me and I wondered what on earth the

person on the other end of the phone said to him. Whatever it was, his eyes twinkled in the light of the room.

"*Oui, un plat de fraises serait formidable. Et maintenez l'ordre de petit-déjeuner jusqu'à dire dix trente.*"

Strawberries in a bowl? Hold breakfast?

"*Chambre neuf quinze.*" Then he hung up with a wink.

The inside of my mouth dried as he advanced toward me.

"The bathroom is through there, in case you want to freshen up."

I nodded, grateful for the opportunity before we got started. Maybe reapply my bright red lipstick and smooth my hair.

Once inside, I closed the door and checked in my purse to make sure I had all the essentials. Phone, condoms in a pouch pack, lipstick, tissues, deodorant, and perfume. Room key and extra contact lenses in a case.

I chanced a look at my burning cheeks. My dress clung to me, outlining every curve. My eyes shone bright, though the contact lenses irritated them a little now and I considered taking them out, but dismissed that plan. "No time, girlie."

My long, blonde hair was still caught up at the nape of my neck, though wisps were escaping. I hadn't brought a comb or brush, so I smoothed them with my hand, noting the slightly startled expression on my face before I turned away.

I used the bathroom quickly, then, after washing my hands, I calmed myself before I walked back into the room, hoping I looked self-possessed and worldly.

A knock on the door caught my attention and I sucked in a deep breath as he answered it. When he came back, he carried a tray with glasses, an ice bucket, a bottle of champagne, and strawberries in a bowl. He smiled at me. I returned the grin.

The pop went off and I giggled nervously.

"You've never done this before, have you?"

I blushed at his question. "Ah, no. Why do you say that?"

"You seem nervous. Then you toy with the clasp on your bag and seem to avoid actually looking at me."

I laughed at that. "Oh, I don't know. I see you standing there." My tummy quivered as I answered with a fair dose of bravado.

His casually spoken words eased my nervousness. "It's not like I'm going to attack you."

He pointed to the balcony. "Come on, let's go outside, check out at the view, and chat."

It really was as if he'd read my mind. So I trailed him out and sat on one of the fine, wrought iron chairs, sipping my champagne and nibbling on the strawberries he'd ordered.

"So... Do you have a name?" I felt a little braver and, to be honest, I think I needed to know at least the first name of the man I was planning on having wild monkey sex with.

"Johnathon."

The name suited him. It was strong and reassuring. I nodded, gazing down on the street. "Do you?" His query startled me and I twisted to look at him.

"Yeah. Davina."

"It's lovely to make your acquaintance, Davina. Would you like a top up?"

"No, thanks. Actually, it's a bit cool." A small breeze had whipped up, and he grabbed

the bowl while I lifted the bottle and we moved back indoors.

The quivering inside me had abated while we'd been sitting outside. Instead, a delicious curl of warmth had invaded my body.

"Shall we…" I stopped. How was the best way to ask this, I wondered.

"Go to bed?" He finished my question and I nodded, suddenly feeling both incredibly shy and gauche.

He smiled and reached for his shirt, unbuttoning it as I watched, then it was gone and his

bronzed chest was bared to my hungry gaze. My panties were damp, my nipples hard buds of need, and I shivered as electrical impulses flashed on and off through my entire being.

"Do you need some help?" he asked.

Oh my God! I'd been standing there watching him while he'd stripped, his pants and boxers gone now, and I was still fully clothed. "Umm…"

He strode toward me, supremely comfortable, I thought, in his skin. The lights were on, the curtains were open, and he was totally naked.

"Can we turn the lights off?" My voice tapered away on a squeak and he winked. "Anything for you."

Once the lights were off, I watched him, my eyes adjusting to the much dimmer surroundings. He reached me and I indicated the zipper at the back of my dress. With exquisite care, he undid the dress so that it gaped, kissing the inches of flesh he uncovered as he went.

I stepped out of the gown and waited for him to finish surveying me in my tiny little black underwear and stockings.

"Very nice." His murmur filled the air and I gulped again.

He watched me, and I didn't know if that made me feel

hotter or more unsure of myself and what I was about to do. My hands shook as I reached for the snaps of my stockings and I felt the drag as the silk dropped away, baring my leg.

"Have you..." My face flamed. Was it even okay to ask? Yes. After all, I was about to have sex with a total stranger and didn't want to pick up anything nasty. "Have you done this before?"

He grinned and a boyish dimple at the side of his mouth flashed. It left me spinning into space as his eyes twinkled. "No. But there's a first time for everything." Then his mouth descended, crushing his lips against mine.

I shivered as his fingers moved to the clips of my bra and I felt the second he had it undone, even though I was mashed against him. The play of his tongue against mine was wickedly arousing and his taste... There was a hint of red wine, some beer. And he was definitely all man.

We sidled to the bed. His erection dug against my belly as he pushed me down. The coolness of the satin comforter touched my scorching skin. The dip of the bed was silent. It was about the only thing my beleaguered brain could accept before it was lost in the whirl of sensations. I did manage to grasp the knowledge that he was obviously well schooled in the art of lovemaking, however.

I gripped onto him, my fingers tracing the sinewy strength of his shoulders.

His hands cupped my breasts, plumped them eagerly, and I sighed, aware of the hot dampness down below at the entrance to my core. I had to work at keeping myself from wrapping my legs around him and impaling myself firmly on his cock.

"Oh, Johnathon." I couldn't help myself. The sexual hunger had been gnawing at me since before I'd met him. Now it flared like a star in its death throes, and all I wanted was for him to bury his body deep within me. I squirmed and he chuckled quietly. Then it stopped.

"You're hot." His mouth closed over mine before I could scream out that I needed to be filled hilt deep.

"Condom." My fingers snagged one of the foil packets and it toppled to the bed. He grabbed it up, tore the corner with his teeth, and quickly sheathed himself. The whole time his gaze burned me with its intensity. It was the most erotic thing I'd ever seen in my life.

His fingers roamed, finding every sweat-slicked inch of my body. I burned beneath his touch; my hips undulated, letting him know I was ready.

He ignored my wordless entreaty, while his lips traced a path down my body, and I groaned as the excitement wound around me, liquid silver flashing through my veins. His mouth reached the indentation at my stomach and I called out to him. "Johnathon!" This time I captured him with my legs, stilling his wandering movements.

I don't want the first time to be his mouth on me as I come to a screaming climax. Oh no! I needed satisfaction and I needed it now. This was my weekend of pleasure and I'd be damned if I'd wait any longer. But I wanted it to be deeply satisfying in a way oral sex could never quite achieve.

I opened my eyes, reached down, and tugged him back toward me. "Fill. Me."

He grinned as he fitted himself against my pussy. I wriggled, looking for the most comfortable position as he started to slowly enter my body.

"Faster."

My demand was met with a frown and he said, "We don't have to hurry."

But I was in desperate need of release. I needed to feel

him moving within me. The emptiness ached, and the only way to assuage it was to be joined with another. "Please."

He slid home and all I could think was I'd never been this full before.

He moved. No more than a tiny nudge, but it opened me to a world of sensation. My breasts rubbed against his chest, his hands found their way beneath my hips and lifted them slightly, and I moaned again. "Oh God!"

"You want more?" Once again he chuckled, and I felt the vibrations through my whole body. It stole my breath and my senses. My sex clenched hard and I nearly went supernova in that instant.

"Yes." My hands tangled in the linen sheets, gripping tightly as I moaned at each movement. The nudges became surging movements and my hips moved in time, thrusting and undulating in his embrace. Our fingers slipped on sweaty skin, but we didn't stop.

The maelstrom grew inside me and I welcomed it. I needed it. The climax rushed over me like a tidal wave of nerve endings releasing while my body stilled, holding me on the precipice of ecstasy. Down I went, letting my body settle while Johnathon pounded into me. His hips see-sawed back and forth until finally he too stopped. His face was statue-like, held in the second of orgasm, and I watched, awed that it was me with whom he shattered.

We slumped together, hearts beating like tom-tom drums, and let the lethargy of after-sex consume us. My body had that heavy after exertion feeling, and I was sure all my bones had melted.

He rolled off me, but cuddled in against my exhausted body, spooning around me. A sensation of wellbeing spread through me and I let it claim me while my eyes weighed heavily, and I couldn't help myself...I slept.

CHAPTER TWO

When I woke, the light filtered into my eyes and I groaned, rolling until I hit something warm and hard. Oh. My. God! For a moment, a dizzying wave of disorientation crashed down on me and I gulped.

I slipped to the side of the bed, thinking only to dress and get out of there before he woke. "Are you planning on leaving immediately?" That lazy voice caught me unaware. "Uhhh..." I couldn't look at him. To do so would probably end up with me staying. I needed to head back to my room and regroup. I hadn't expected the sex to be so great or to feel so out of control afterward.

Even as I stood and searched for my clothes, the thoughts hammered at me. I pushed them away, hunting for my garments. The delicious little black dress I wore the night before, where the hell was it? I caught sight of the black material where it lay on the floor, crumpled like yesterday's newspaper. I grimaced at the thought of wearing it in the hotel down to my room. An evening gown worn in the morning would be the biggest giveaway, and surely people would know what I had been up to.

A rustle of fabric heralded movement and I glanced up as strong hands settled on my shoulder. "You aren't embarrassed, are you, Davina?"

I turned and I could see that he knew from the expression on his face. "I...uhhh..." I gulped and the sound carried, while he smiled, that wicked dimple peeking out.

"Come on. Before you go, join me for breakfast. It can't be too far away." He turned, I guessed to check the clock at the bedside. "It's due here in twenty minutes. While we're waiting, I'll make you a tea... Or are you a coffee girl?"

Oh God! I don't do morning-afters. For heaven's sake, he doesn't even know if I drink coffee or tea. What kind of a woman did that make me? Cheap. Easy. A one-night-stand girl, my brain offered unhelpfully, and I swallowed the wail that rose in my throat. "I like coffee. White, but no sugar."

"Excellent. A woman after my own heart. Go hop in the shower and soak away your worries."

With an anxious nod I gave in, scurrying for the bathroom. My eyes ached and itched as I realized I still had my contacts in. "Damn."

"What's up?"

A jerky turn had me looking back, and I realized I'd said the word aloud. "I left my contacts in. I have another pair in my bag." The words ended with a note of hysteria and I cringed.

"I'll find your bag. You just go shower and I'll pop it in the bathroom for you."

"Thank you." I sucked in an unsteady breath, hoping it would calm me down just a little. My belly jiggled with nerves, and the more I thought about it, I really felt like I needed to get clean. But was it a skin deep clean I needed or something more?

Right now I didn't want to focus on the negatives in my

life. I was there to have a great time, get laid, and see Paris at its best. Well, I'd already achieved one, and if I could somehow talk him into it, perhaps he might stick around for the whole weekend. So I ignored that insistent tapping at my brain that said this wasn't necessarily the brightest choice and scurried into the bathroom. Once the door was closed, I got into the luxurious shower and turned on the water.

The pressure was low, one of the things I missed from Australia. I used the complimentary shampoo and conditioner, working my hair into a lather before rinsing it out, then, finally clean, I flicked off the tap.

Realizing that once again I had forgotten to remove my contacts, I reached for a fluffy towel, but instead it was slipped around me.

"Uh..."

"Hi there." Soft lips found mine and I couldn't control the streak of desire that suffused me once again.

When he finally moved back, I cast around. "I was just about to..."

"Remove your contacts?"

I nodded, quite disconcerted that he seemed to know what I was thinking and about to say before I did.

"No worries. I found the lens case and popped it onto the side here for you."

"Oh. Oh, well..." He'd found it in my bag? What else had he seen? I wasn't so sure I liked that as a concept, but it was done, and I was in his room, after all.

"Your bag wasn't closed properly and everything spilled out all over the floor." Now I felt pretty low, as if he'd read my thoughts yet again.

"Thanks." I pulled the towel closer around myself, feeling more than just naked at the situation I had put myself in. I wasn't altogether sure I could cope. My hands shook wildly. "Do you mind if..." I didn't look at him, but felt the heat of a fully fledged blush creeping over my face and chest.

"Uh, yeah. I'll just..." He left the room and that sensation of being uncomfortable floated through me again, as if I were coming to terms with my own bad decision.

I removed the old lenses and blinked rapidly several times before applying the new ones. My eyes itched and hurt, but I needed to be able to see where I was going and what I was about to do.

The muffled sounds of chatter came from the room, so I hesitated, trying to wait out the time until whoever was beyond left. Then I sucked in every ounce of confidence I had and stepped out of the bathroom, wrapped in the large, white, terry cloth bath towel. I looked around the corner, seeing my clothing arranged on the bed neatly. I almost blushed again and scurried over, reaching for my clothes.

"Would you like to join me for breakfast?"

This time when I turned around he smiled at me and I nearly swallowed my tongue. In that instant, I longed to do anything I could with this man.

"Uh..." I shook my head. "I should head back to my room."

He smiled. "Why? Is breakfast going to be waiting for you there?" That stopped me. Oh my. I hadn't really thought any of this out, had I?

"Would you like to spend the day with me?"

I was sitting opposite Johnathon in one of the deep, cushy pink seats, eating hot, buttery croissants, and drinking latte when he spoke. I jumped a little, spilling a drop on my robe, and he sighed.

"Sorry, I didn't mean to surprise you."

"No. It's okay." I patted away at the drips, feeling foolish. "I'm not used to..."

He reached out and placed a warm and well-manicured hand on mine. The warmth of his touch filled me once more with longing. "It's fine."

I swallowed. Here was the man I'd slept with, had wild sex with, and I was as nervous as a virgin on her wedding night. Damn. This isn't the way it should play out!

"Yeah. I'd love to spend the day with you." The words escaped on a croak, but once said, that was it. I was committed.

"Fantastic. What would you like to do? Go for a walk? Visit the Louvre?"

"A walk would be fantastic. But..." I broke off, once more the now familiar burning blush creeping over my skin. "Err...I need to go back to my room and change." I glanced up at him and saw the smile on his face.

"Sounds great."

I pushed away from the table. "I'm in room five-four-teen. If you want to come down..." Johnathon had seen my distraction, and risen. He folded his arms around me and I leaned in, inhaling his scent. Masculine and warm. I couldn't resist his lips as they joined mine. My senses flew as he laid claim to me, his scorching touch setting my body aflame.

I'm not even totally sure how he achieved it. One minute I was in his arms, the next I was naked on the bed with him again. I tugged on the cloth covering his body, all of a sudden so hungry to feel the warm flesh beneath my grasp.

His lips traced a path over my jaw and down my throat and I groaned, unable to stop the sound erupting inside me. "Oh, Johnathon."

Down they trailed, finding my chest and breasts. The overload of sensations nearly shattered the small bit of consciousness that I clung to. He suckled one nipple then the other, the tip of his tongue sliding around the rapidly budding areola, and I had to gasp. My body arched into him, eager to experience more of his delightfully erotic lovemaking.

My fingers twined in the fluffy tie and finally, with pulling and jerking, I freed the small knot and his robe hung free. Now I could repay his caresses.

I slipped my hand over his stomach, and his muscles clenched beneath the gliding touch. He hissed and I wanted to grin. "Oh yes, this is fun, isn't it?"

He muttered something unintelligible before his mouth slid back to mine.

My hands fluttered further south, finding the crisp hairs at the junction to his thigh. His erection stood proud, jutting out, and I grasped it. The feel of that satiny smooth hardness filled me with a sense of power. When he tore his mouth away from mine I propelled myself toward his groin. I wanted to taste him, to feel that length in my mouth. I did just that, bending my head down to him so I could suck him as far in as I could. I moved over him while his hands gripped my head, helping me to find the rhythm of movement. His hips swayed as I sucked and licked.

My hands shook as I carefully encircled his sac, gently playing with it while he hissed and moved faster and harder, his thrusts deeper with each pass. He pulled away and a pop sounded. The only other sound was the frantic rustle of fabric and pants as we heaved, searching for breath and a condom.

He shoved me back, his hand urgent and ungentle as I tumbled back to the softness of the bed. I knew what he wanted. Hell, I wanted it too. I lifted my legs, shivering while the warm air caressed my wet and very ready intimate skin. His fingers brushed through the damp hairs. His erection rubbed against me, and he whispered, "You are so beautiful."

Then he pushed in. The burning sensation of stretching left me gasping. I arched, knowing my breasts were displayed for him, but I couldn't watch, my eyes heavy with desire fluttered closed. The movement of his hands left me shaking as he set to plucking my nipples before I clenched my legs around his hips.

He slid and slipped within me, the undulation more like waves on the shore, battering at me once again as I bowed upward. My heart pounded in my chest and the sounds of slapping flesh mingled with sighs and groans. Scent, heavy and musky, filled the air and I breathed, my body demanding more oxygen. Every subtle action of our lovemaking wound the spring inside me tighter.

We moved in some unheard rhythm, my hands now reaching out, looking for him. "Johnathon." I heard my voice, but it sounded different. My hands settled on his arms. His lips covered mine as he surged within me again.

This time he found that spot, deep inside my body, and I started tingling. My climax was close as he moved again. I moaned against his mouth and he swallowed the sounds I made.

One last momentous thrust pushed us both over the edge. His fingers dug into my hips while my legs gripped him. The exquisite feel of my body working at him overwhelmed my senses. Then thought splintered and fled.

THIS TIME, WHEN I ROLLED OFF THE BED I KNEW I couldn't hang around any longer. Johnathon

lay there, impressively naked, while I hunted for stockings and underwear and quickly donned them. I gripped my bag in my hand. He kept grinning at me the whole time and my body felt flushed and hot after that latest round of sweaty lovemaking. "I'm going down to my room to shower and change. Come down in about half an hour." He quirked and eye and my stomach tripped over itself. "Please?"

I wasn't even sure why I was pleading with him, just that I didn't want this connection to end here. So I waited, swallowing the roiling nerves that jiggled in my belly. He inclined his head and I breathed a sigh of relief. Pleasure speared me, knowing that our association, whatever it might be, wasn't over just yet.

I finished dressing, hastily slipping into my little black dress. The tiny black bra from last night was stuffed into my bag which bulged at its addition. Thankfully, I wasn't too large, so it was okay to go braless every now and again.

With a quick smile in his direction, I scurried for the door, bending down to collect the lovely black shoes I'd worn last night. I beat a retreat. Once the door shut behind me, I stopped, leaned against the wall for a moment, and closed my eyes, struggling for some inner calm before I pushed away.

I raced for the elevator and slipped in. The car held several people, and an older couple eyed me. I knew I must have looked a fright with tousled hair, shoes in hand, and bulging evening bag, so I tried to avoid their gaze as much as possible. But the knowledge that I'd had hot, steamy sex with a man I'd only met hours ago ate at me.

My floor arrived soon enough and I hurried out of the elevator, but the woman's comment, "Did you see that? Wanton hussy," rang in my ears as I moved down the hall at a rapid pace.

Once inside my room, I stopped and anger poured through me. How dare that woman judge me? But the truth was I probably judged myself far more harshly than she ever could.

With a quick flick, I threw my bag on the bed and raced around the room, raiding my suitcase for jeans, shirt, and my favorite boots. I scurried into the bathroom, showered quickly again, and got dressed. I scraped my hair back into a ponytail and set about applying minimal makeup. "What the hell compelled you to plan this weekend?" But even as I asked myself that question, looking critically in the mirror, I knew why.

Because I was turning thirty and there was no man on the horizon for me. A deep sigh loosed from my chest. That was the truth. I was getting older and was firmly on the shelf, to use the terminology of regency romance.

There was no use dwelling on the negatives. Johnathon, the sexiest and most amazing lover I'd ever had, would be here soon. "Come on, girl. Time to finish getting ready before he arrives."

I had just finished zipping the side closure of my boots when a knock came at the door. I fished my backpack from the suitcase, flipped the lid close, and headed for the door.

He smiled as I opened the door and I melted again. "Hi."

"Hi. Come in. I'm nearly ready."

He followed me in, shut the door, and sat down on the bed while I grabbed all the

necessities and shoved them into my backpack. Last up, I threw in the room key and smiled brightly. "I'm ready. Where to?"

His grin was infectious. "I thought we'd go find a small restaurant for lunch and get to know each other a little bit."

My heart fluttered in my chest. Get to know me? In usual relationship terms, I knew that meant seeing if there was the possibility of enough to have a long-term relationship. Did that mean...

Perhaps I shouldn't think like that though. After all, this was only meant to be a sexy weekend tryst, nothing more. Yet, no matter how hard I tried to tell myself this, more yearning and hopeful thoughts occurred to me. Then came another. Visions of this handsome man at my side, meeting my parents, coming home to a glass of wine and a shared dinner filled me with warmth. Nights in front of the television, snuggled up together. My heart stuttered.

"Davina?"

I looked at him hoping he couldn't read the fear and longing on my face. "Yeah, let's just go."

I turned away, not wanting to face the questions that he would ask, or the need that I felt in that instant. In silence, we left the room and wandered into the hall, then, slipping our arms through each other's, we headed to the elevators. This time they were empty and we travelled together without speaking. I was thankful for that. I didn't want to talk. I just needed to clear my head before lunch. We headed through the lobby and out onto the street.

Glorious Paris sunshine shone down and I basked in the sense of wellbeing that came with it.

"You like Paris, don't you?" Johnathon spoke quietly and I turned. "I love it. There's nothing like this at home."

"New Zealand?"

I coughed and shook my head before pinning him with a mock scowl. "Wash your mouth out! I'm from Queensland, Australia."

He lifted both hands in mock surrender. "I give in."

I giggled and he slung his arm around my shoulder. "I haven't been there in a long, long time. So you can tell me about it over lunch."

We walked until we found a small restaurant that appealed to us, taking seats by the window. Over lunch we talked about my family and the small farm in the hinterlands of Brisbane. How, even though my parents were small crops farming, I didn't really feel it was my future. I told him about my siblings, my flighty baby brother, and how I'd ended up in London on a temporary placement that had become semi-permanent.

We laughed and I learned Johnathon had a biting wit. He was adroit at mimicry and by the end of the meal, he was giving me an impressive rendition of our obsequious waiter. But he never spoke of himself or his past.

The only thing which dampened our time together were the men who seemed to watch us discreetly. "Uh, Johnathon?" He smiled at me and I melted deep inside. "Why do you think those guys are watching us?"

"They aren't watching us. We're just tourists. Probably some foreign dignitary is in town, looking to lay low or here for some kind of break."

His words didn't really feel right, but I accepted them at face value. We were just two normal people enjoying the sunshine in Paris, weren't we?

As we left the table, one of the men lifted a newspaper

and I wanted to laugh at myself for the silly whimsy. I slung my bag over my shoulder and off we trotted, heading for the Seine. I'd been there a couple of times before, but always on my own. Somehow, having someone to share the experience with made it seem more meaningful. I snorted, and when Johnathon looked at me, I read the question in his eyes.

"Oh, daft thoughts. Nothing to waste our time on."

He frowned, but I tugged him along. Thankfully, the pathways weren't crowded on this Friday afternoon. I was fairly sure the following day there would be a constant flow of people. Here and there lovers sat, entwined around each other, street musicians played, and the irregular, older artists touting their paintings caught my eye.

One in particular was gorgeous. A charcoal of the view in front of us. Before my mesmerized gaze, the old man drew slashes on the paper, each new inch of line work revealing another aspect of the vista. At the end, he turned and said something in rapid fire French and Johnathon grinned broadly before reaching into his pocket. Money changed hands and the image was carefully packaged and handed to Johnathon. He slipped his arm through mine and we strode away.

The further we walked, the more of Paris opened to my eyes, but I didn't feel the ache of my feet or my rising thirst until we sat down at a corner cafe. Two drinks were ordered and Johnathon offered the painting to me.

"It's gorgeous. What will you do with it?" I couldn't help the question, and he smiled, but this time it didn't reach his eyes.

"It's not for me. It's for you. So when our time together is ended, you won't forget me."

For me? I sucked in a deep breath. "But…" The words wouldn't come though. Was our time coming to an end that quickly? I'd barely begun getting to know him. Then I stopped myself. That was never the plan, was it? A weekend of sex was all I had signed up for.

The coffees arrived and we drank in silence as sadness and loss filled me. It didn't feel right, but why? Why did it feel so wrong? I didn't know the answer.

The walk back to the hotel was slower, more difficult. I felt that gap between us widening, and mourned it. "Are you leaving soon?" I stopped him at the great glass doors to the hotel and hoped he wouldn't say yes.

His brow crinkled slightly and I wanted to reach up and smooth those worry lines away. He sighed heavily. "Not today. Maybe not even tomorrow, but it depends on my staff. I don't know when."

Because the intimacy between us was so new, I wasn't sure what his reaction would be, but I wound my arms around his waist, sinking into his embrace. His arms wrapped around me, and I soaked up the warmth he exuded and the male scent.

"Spend the night with me?" His soft whisper called to me. Each second we spent together would make saying goodbye harder, I knew that on a purely intellectual level. But I couldn't let go. Not yet. That knowledge tore at me, clawing my inside with razor sharp efficiency.

My eyes teared, but I nodded. "Yeah. I'd like to." I heard the thickness of my voice and suddenly that hunger roared to life again and I grabbed his hand, hauling him through the doors, across the lobby, and into the elevator. As the door closed, I noticed it was empty, so I pulled his face down toward me. The curling, simmering heat flowed through my bones like molten molasses as I devoured his mouth, tasting his muskiness deep within that wet, warm cavern.

My hands twined in the sandy blond hair, so soft, and the stubble on his cheeks scraped me. A dim ding intruded my passionate fog and I lifted my head. "Our floor," I croaked. Well, his floor, but right now I didn't care.

I hurried to the door, looking at him, and he no doubt read the urgency on my face. His own was graven, while his eyes blazed with hunger. Barely had he swiped the card in the reader than we shoved open the door and it slammed with my body hard against it.

I didn't care. I needed him. I needed to feel his body moving within me to soothe the savagely hungry beast that overtook my senses.

Our lips and tongues met and mated once more. This time I swung my legs around his hips and he crowded me, the feel of his erection hard against my hungry belly.

CHAPTER THREE

My hands tore at his shirt, several buttons popping and flying, but neither of us stopped what we were doing. The second I had my hands on the smooth, satiny skin of his chest, I ran my thumbs over his small, brown nipples. They grew hard beneath my ministrations and I tweaked them once, twice, and then again.

He gasped into my mouth, but his tongue slid along mine, filled my head with the taste of him. I let my fingers glide over his shoulders and held on, this time flexing my legs in a parody of the most carnal act of all.

He moved. Surged toward the bed where we fell to its softness with an oof. He reared back. "I want you naked. Hot and naked."

I shuddered, pulling at my shirt, tearing the soft cotton while he watched me, eyes as thin as slits, his cheekbones crested red.

His jerky movements as he pulled his arms from his shirt told me how aroused he was, but I didn't care, because I wanted him just as fiercely. I tugged my shirt over my head, my hair catching, and I hissed as a second of pain ripped through my scalp.

"Let me." He leaned forward, pulling my hair slightly to the side as he spoke, and the innate scent of him wove around me, calling to me on a purely primal level. I sucked it in, as his arms continued down my back to find the two clasps that held my bra closed. He brushed the straps over my shoulders and drew the wispy lace away from my skin.

"You have the most beautiful breasts." The breathlessness of his voice filled me with overwhelming emotion.

"Well, I have to say, your chest is pretty impressive too." I moved to scooch to the end of the bed, but he stopped me.

"No. I need to love you this time."

The meaning of his words floated through me. "You mean..."

He nodded and the wickedness in his smile stole my breath. "Now just lie back and let me do the work for a while."

Goosebumps rose on my flesh and my nipples puckered almost painfully as he reached for the zips on my boots. First he raised the left leg, running his hand up over the knee, the denim catching and rolling slightly in the most erotic way. He rubbed right up to the waistband, the muscles of my stomach contracted, then he winked and slid them back down again, before capturing the tab and pulling on it. By the time the boot was gone I was panting with excitement.

He did the same on the other side and my heart pounded in my chest. "Oh, Johnathon..."

I wanted to ask him to come to me, but he grinned, that damned dimple flashing as he must have read the question in my eyes.

My mouth dried when he placed both hands on my

calves and rubbed up again, both hands together. My senses went into overdrive, the lids of my eyes became too heavy, and I panted loudly to my sensitized hearing.

His hands reached my belly, gently caressed, and I clenched the muscles, but he laughed gently. "Let's get these off you."

He reached for and unfastened the snap, unzipping my pants, then rolling the denim off my legs. Then, there I was in nothing but a tiny little thong I'd chosen that morning. It covered next to nothing, and was all that lay between his now questing fingers and my most secret recesses.

I knew they were damp. I could smell my own arousal on the air, and when he reached down, I was sure I was going to die of embarrassment. He hooked a finger through the crotch and tugged. Just a little, so they slid infinitesimally uncovering just the top of my mound.

"Pretty pussy," he crooned, kissing just above the elastic waistband.

I moaned at his onslaught. His finger moved back and forth, still hidden with the crotch and ever so gently grazing my core. "Oh God!" Unable to contain the excitement rising within me, I threw my head back, my breasts pushed forward.

"I love your breasts, but right now, what I want is here."

I felt that tug again, and this time my panties slipped further down my legs while the brush of his breath over my exposed flesh left me a quivering mass of wildly clenching nerve endings. When his tongue swiped over that newly uncovered area, I bucked. The emptiness deep within my core yearned once more to be filled.

"Please. Inside me..." My words were little more than a broken whisper, but he must have ignored that as he opened me with two fingers. I felt the movement, gentle but inexorable, and then his tongue found that tiny nub between my legs, flicked it, and I was sure I saw stars.

"Ah!"

The flick came again, searing my senses.

"Oh, please!"

Again his fingers worked quickly, deftly slipping within the folds, filling me. Not what I wanted, but they moved, finding that tiny point within my body. They rubbed up and down, in and out, and my senses fled, my legs clenched convulsively while I groaned and arched.

"Please."

He moved faster, his mouth now fastened over me, suckling and licking, while he murmured words so sensually erotic they added another layer to the storm that crashed upon me. "You taste like honey and spice."

My thighs started to quiver and joined with the tension that coiled within my core. Heat seared my body and I knew I was close to orgasm. "Johnathon? Please?"

"Let go. Let me taste you. Every bit of you." His breath dusted my skin and it was the final act that pushed me over the edge. My body exploded, and I climaxed with a cry as he slipped his fingers from deep inside my body and his mouth worked at me. Then I dropped through the layers of consciousness as my body rested.

Fingers skated over my skin and I moved again. My mouth was dry and my nerves totally shot. Just like they would be after a heavy night at a bachelors and spinsters ball. I must have muttered it out loud, because I heard him laugh before he gave one more lick on my quivering flesh. "God, you taste good!"

No one had ever said that before, but I kept my mouth firmly shut on that thought. His hands released their grip on my hips. There would probably be bruises, but I didn't care. That had to be the most amazing climax of my life. His mouth didn't stop and neither did his wonderfully clever fingers, they stoked over my belly and I reached for him.

"Not yet," he whispered against my belly button, and then darted in with his tongue and I had to catch my breath.

"I want..."

He laughed. "I'll give you what you want soon."

The need that never left when I was around him curled again, but I was done being passive. I swung my legs around his waist, gripped his shoulders, and rolled. His oof filled my ears, but now I lay over him and my hunger was ratcheting up once more. My legs straddled his chest and I looked down into his face.

"My turn, big boy."

He barked a laugh as I wriggled down his body leaving a damp, musky trail on him.

I considered it, that trail. My essence, his taste. Nothing left to lose. Quickly, I ducked my head and licked him.

"Do you like that?" The tension in his voice stopped me.

"Like what?" I wasn't totally sure what he meant and blushed, the scorching heat searing my face.

"Our tastes. Together."

My eyes widened then I grinned. "Yeah. You taste damned good."

I kissed him fully on the mouth and his tongue darted in and out in the parody of the sexy scene we'd acted out before. I groaned and his hands caught at my hips, pushing me down his body.

I tore my mouth away. "Not yet. My turn."

His movements stilled and his chest labored. He was hot and aroused, but I had just a little bit more to push him to the edge. With a swing of my leg, I was off him and he watched, laying his hands on the bed cover.

"Good. Keep them there."

He quirked a brow, but waited silently as I dropped my head toward his engorged cock. I blew lightly, watching the way it jerked beneath my teasing. He hissed and I swiped it lightly with my tongue. He shook, but held himself still. His muscles locked as if he had to fight some deep inner battle to not take control.

Once more I licked at him, this time longer and harder. The salty secretion at the tip told me he wouldn't last long. I closed my mouth over his head and then slid down his shaft. All the way.

He bucked and I sucked hard, running my tongue around the steely softness before sliding back up, then thrusting down over him again.

This time Johnathon cried out while his fingers curled claw-like into the bedding. "Davina? I can't hold on much longer." I could hear it in his laboring voice, but just a little more would be all I could manage too, as my own insides melted and my body prepared itself for his intimate invasion.

"We should use a condom." His groan filled my senses, but I needed to taste him, just a little more. So I suckled. Harder.

Each thrust tied me up, accentuated the emptiness inside me. The muscles of my pussy

quivered with need as I moved, my breasts swinging slightly, making me gasp, and I let go. He grabbed at a small foil packet, tore it, and rolled it over his engorged flesh.

He shoved me to the bed, his mouth rapacious. My breast in his mouth, his fingers shoving home between my legs, and my mouth nibbling at his sweaty skin.

Primal lust took over. We moved against each other, cries of hunger filling the air, and the scent heady in the Parisian dusk.

Finally, he settled between my thighs, pushing them apart. I had no recollection of how we got into that position, but I needed his cock embedded firmly within my pussy. The tip nudged me, scalding the flesh before it slowly eased inside.

I was slick and ready and he slipped home inch by inch. He held himself hilt deep as I captured his waist between my thighs and clutched tightly.

"Move, damn you." I grunted and he did. Rocking deeply, skin against skin. Each stroke hard and fast, shattering me so completely.

"I love the feel of you. So hot. So tight." Our fingers laced as he called my name, and then he shoved one more time, hitting that spot while I arched, unable to contain the scream, and he joined me, echoing my release.

I felt the muted jetting deep within and the sensation was right and necessary.

We stayed still, lost in our embrace. It could have been hours or years. Most likely it was only minutes as our breathing settled back into a slower rhythm. The only thing I knew for certain was I'd never experienced anything like that before. I probably never would again, if I wasn't with him.

"Oh God, Johnathon. What are we going to do?"

He pulled away, slumped to the side where he lay on his back, arm flung over his eyes. "I don't know." His muttered words washed over me. Cold and empty.

My weekend tryst had become something so much more. But in the process it had become so much less. I lay there, tears trickling down my face.

I'd really fucked it up this time. I'd fallen in love with a man I'd met not even twenty-

four hours before. What the hell am I going to do? But there was no answer.

GLOOM DESCENDED AND I ROSE, QUIETLY, TAKING CARE not to wake Johnathon. I knew he was asleep as he snored lightly. I cast around thinking to grab my clothes and get out of there. I'd already made a prize fool of myself once over a man. I didn't need to add to that.

My panties lay on the floor and I scooped them up, slipped them on, and hunted for my bra, jeans, and shirt. The jeans lay on the carpet and a boot nearby. I picked them up. My heart beat wildly in my chest as I looked toward the bed, but the sound came as rhythmically as before.

My blouse was nowhere to be found, so I slid open his wardrobe, picked out the first top I could find and donned it. I hastily buttoned up and pushed my legs into the heavy denim of my pants. My bag was still on the floor where it had fallen, forgotten, and I tugged on it. The painting was still rolled up in the tube and my boots were in the corner. I grabbed them before letting myself out quietly.

Tears stung my eyes as I scurried toward the elevator. "Not now," I whispered fiercely and waited impatiently for the lift to slide open. Then I stepped inside, pushed the button, and the ancient cage descended.

When it reached the fifth floor, the door slid open and,

without looking one way or the other, I headed to my own room, fishing in the pocket of the bag for my key card.

Inside, I dropped to the ground and the tears flowed. My chest bellowed with grief. "Oh my God. What have I done?"

I couldn't contain the misery or anguish any longer. Johnathon was the man I'd been searching for. For thirty years, the one for me had been on the other side of the globe. And all he would remember of me was the hot weekend of meaningless sex.

I couldn't stay any longer. That much I knew. Because to stay would make this situation intolerable for me. With that single thought, I opened my suitcase, stripped off his shirt and gently folded it, slipping it into my suitcase. Then I found a bra and blouse, promising myself to throw any of the ones I'd worn with him in the bin when I got home.

I hurried around, gathering my items. Rushing into the small bathroom, I thrust my toiletries into the case, zipped it up with brutal efficiency, and willed myself not to cry any further.

Then I slumped onto my bed and sobbed as if my world had ended, which on some levels, it had. Afterward, spent, I lay there listlessly. I wondered if he'd woken and realized I'd left. Probably not, I told myself with ruthless truth.

"Stop dreaming. It's time to go home to your empty life. The one you chose, remember?"

With those words, I got off the bed and hauled on the handle of the case and headed for the door. Even as I wrenched it open I felt a surge of regret.

There he stood, in the doorway.

"Where are you going?" he asked.

My heart began to beat faster, being near to him.

"Home." I didn't want to have this conversation with him. Not now. I was fragile.

Bruised. Damaged on a level I'd never experienced before. He blanched and I grimaced.

"Look. It was a totally hot weekend. Right?"

He seemed lost. "Weekend? It's barely started. It's only..." He glanced at his watch. "...three in the morning."

A blow to my solar plexus couldn't have knocked the wind out of my sails any more efficiently. "Shit."

"What?" He leaned in and I wanted so badly to kiss him, to wind my arms around him. But I couldn't.

"We met twenty-four hours ago."

He sighed. "So you're running away because of that?"

That stung. He was close to the bone and didn't know it. "No."

He stared at me and I blushed.

"Yes."

He quirked an eyebrow.

"I don't know. Okay? I just don't know."

He reached out, cupping my face. "Maybe we need to talk."

I laughed. "We did that earlier. And that ended up in sex."

He winced. "Not... Look, not like that, okay?"

"What do you propose? The restaurants will be closed now and I'm hungry. You probably are too." My stomach rumbled, reminding me we'd skipped dinner, somehow.

"Put your bag back in the hotel room and we can go down to the bar. They serve light meals."

I nodded. I was hungry and now he was here. I couldn't see how I could possibly ignore his plea. So I didn't. I pushed the bag back into the room, dumping it front of the bathroom door, and he sighed.

"Okay," he muttered and reached for my hand. I let him hold it and usher me to the elevator.

This time, when we entered, we separated. I remembered the time before and so did he, I was sure, as his face flamed. I couldn't look at him, which felt weird after what we had done to each other in the last twenty-four hours. Then I shrugged. Not much else for it, was there?

The doors slid open and we got out. He took my hand once more and led me out onto the street. It was almost silent, but the lamps still glowed dimly as we made our way to the scene of our meeting. That little bar was lit gaily as we entered. The ding of the bell filled the air. Without a word, we headed to the corner seats where I had sat the night before.

The bar tender looked up, a startled look on his face before a veil settled over his gaze and he reached for the wine I'd been drinking and a beer for Johnathon.

Only once the drinks sat on the table before us did he pick up the menu. It was sparse, but I wasn't really hungry now. I settled for a croissant filled with creamy chicken, as did he. The order was taken quickly and we waited in relative silence for it to be delivered to the table.

"So, where do I start?"

I cocked my head at his words. "The beginning usually works as well as anything." He laughed.

"You're uncomfortable, aren't you?" It wasn't the most amazing opening ever, but he

nodded with a jerk.

"I, umm. It's hard to explain." He squirmed in his chair and I wondered why he was so ill at ease. He gazed over my shoulder. "What's up?"

He blushed and it was endearing, even while it left me

feeling oddly awkward. What could be so bad that he can't tell me, I wondered.

"Umm, my people." He nodded and I turned in my chair, seeing the men from the restaurant. His people?

"What do you mean? Your people?" Confusion filled me along with wariness.

"I own this big business. It's a financial house."

My stomach curdled. I really didn't want to know where this was going. I knew what the financial world was like, insular. Very few women engaged in relationships with those higher up, but those who did were often ostracized for sleeping their way to the top. I was happy at the middle management level. I enjoyed my job.

"So which company?" I needed to know which one, because it would mean the end of our alliance. "Oh, and explain the 'your people' thing too, please."

He huffed heavily. "My people. Because of who I am, it's hard to enjoy a weekend or break on my own. I'm always surrounded by minders and staff. It gets wearing."

"Why? Why are you always surrounded?"

"Money. Apparently, I'm an ideal kidnap target. So wherever I go, I'm surrounded by minders. This time we agreed I would take a holiday, but surrounded, without them impinging on me."

I frowned, not really liking what he was telling me or the truths that he'd hidden. "So in the restaurant then? They really were your people? The ones reading the newspapers?"

He nodded and the sense of betrayal lanced through me. He lied to me. On some level, my brain told me I was overreacting. After all, this was only ever meant to be a weekend tryst.

"Where else were your people?"

He winced at my bald demand. But I was angry. That seed had grown into a blazing conflagration as he'd spoken. I couldn't accept lies from the men I engaged in any kind of relationship with.

"At the hotel. I, um... I own it. And this bar. I own it too."

My fists clenched. I'd been taken for a long foolish ride. Hell, I'd taken myself for a long foolish ride and enjoyed it along the way.

"Where. Else?"

"Davina..." He leaned over, extending his hand to mine, but I pulled them out of his reach. Hurt settled on his face, but right now I just didn't care.

"Tell. Me." My teeth gritted so hard they almost hurt, and he sank back in his seat, a frown marring his profile.

"Several followed us along the riverbank too."

That was enough. I'd heard as much as I could take, pushed my chair back, and stood with a jerk. "I can't do this. No more. You lied to me."

He followed me as I headed for the door. "Wait. Davina, wait!"

The bloody long-legged blonde he'd come in with the previous night was sitting in the corner, shrinking from my gaze, obviously trying not to watch or be seen. The ache that started in my belly rose up and clawed at my chest. "Was she involved?"

I whirled back toward him; he cannoned into me, winding his arms around me as I hissed the demanding question. I pointed to the super chic French woman and he nodded.

"You bastard!" He stilled and I tore his hands from me. Anger coursed and my face burned with shame. I'd been right royally played and it was time to call it quits.

"I'm going. Don't follow me. Don't talk to me. I don't want to know." I stalked away, placing my hand on the cool metal handle of the door.

"I'm sorry, Davina."

I heard the whisper, but had to get out of there. My eyes stung with unshed tears, ones I had no intention of allowing him to see. Not after the way I'd been used.

In that instant, I realized I wanted to go home. Not back to some anonymous hotel. I just wanted my own bed, my pillows to grip while I gave into whatever damned emotion this was battering at me.

I hurried to the hotel, made my way quickly to my room, intending nothing more than to grab my bag, check out, and make my way to the airport. I had enough money to be able to grab the next available flight.

A wrench on the door opened the room and there was my bag, exactly where I'd left it. I gripped the handle, vainly clutching onto it in an attempt to block out the pain rippling through me. I raced to the elevator, stepped in, and headed to the ground floor.

I said a silent 'thank you' when there was no one at the desk and I dashed away the tears that fell. Of course that was short lived, as one of the clerks answered the imperious ding of the small brass bell.

"I want to check out." I gave my room number, and the woman tapped on the computer then looked at me with a smile.

"Oh, your bill is already taken care of."

"What? No. I haven't paid my bill yet." I leaned in, but the woman patted my hand.

"Seriously, it's all done. See?"

She swung the screen around so I could see. It had a bright red Paid In Full on the bottom of the screen, and I ground my teeth. Doesn't he realize that makes it worse? But of course not.

He had no idea that I now felt like I'd been paid for services. Turmoil and anguish warred, but I concentrated on breathing deeply. On staying calm. I could let go when I finally entered my flat in London.

Seething , I nodded and headed for the door. "Miss Chandler? Do you want a car?"

I stopped. In my anger, I hadn't even considered how I'd get to the airport. I wasn't going to take his bloody car. But she could order me a taxi.

"Get me a taxi please."

Her smile melted away and on her face there was wariness. But she didn't argue, instead lifting the handle of the phone and ordering transportation for me. When she hung up, she smiled carefully. "It should be waiting outside now. I have been instructed to let them know that we will pay your fare."

God, that just rubbed salt into the wound as I stalked through the lobby and out the door.

CHAPTER FOUR

Even in the cool morning, the airport was loud and busy. I hurried over to the desk, hoping to get any flight possible and head home. If I was lucky, I could be home before dawn. As I scanned the board, my heart dropped in my chest. The next flight of the day would be another couple of hours away at just after six AM. But that flight had a longer duration. If I waited another hour, I could be home some time after peak hour settled. I headed for the desk and the woman looked harried as she smiled at me. "Can I help you?"

"I need a one-way flight to London. The first available flight."

She looked at me and I realized I must look like some kind of wild woman. "Just one moment."

She tapped away at the screen. "I have one seat on the next Brit Air flight. But all I have left is a business class seat."

"I'll take it." While the woman filled out the details, I tapped my foot on the floor, feeling anxious to be away. Finally, ticket in hand and suitcase handed over, I made my way to the business lounge. There I could have a glass of wine or a coffee, if that suited, while I waited for my flight.

The room wasn't cozy, it was too devoid of personality to be called that, but it was quiet, muted really, and I dropped my bag and coat on the first available plush, red seat and headed for the barista.

Cradling my coffee, I settled in to wait. Now and again there were announcements, and I focused on them, hoping to avoid the agony that squeezed my heart. Though I refused to give in to the pain and watched the board, the television, and the people coming and going, it didn't diminish the grief that stole my breath. It stayed there, sneaking up whenever I dropped my defenses.

Even boarding the plane was difficult. I looked out the window, thankful there was no one in the seat beside me. The engines rumbled to life and I turned away, unable to handle the jolt of grief that came with the knowledge that down there, somewhere, was Johnathon. Lying, cheating scumbag that he was, my heart felt as if it had been cleaved in two.

I got through the flight, accepting a hot coffee from the hostess and drinking it during the hour long trip. When we finally landed, I breathed a sigh of relief, and stumbled off the plane. "Thank you," I mumbled to the crew member as I stepped through the portal.

The bags were unloaded. I called for a vehicle to take me home. The sense of numbness was leaching away and the sting of betrayal and loss was there. My eyes burned and my chest thudded rather like a panic attack.

I spied my bag, yanked it from the carousel, and moved quickly, thankful to see my car waiting. I bundled in, gave my address, and then stared determinedly out the window, needing to avoid talking. In my present state of mind I would lose it, I knew.

Finally, the driver deposited me at the door, and as I slipped my key into the lock, the first drips started rolling down my face. "Oh God." The torrent rushed at me and I had to hurry. The key slid out of the lock, scraping over my knuckles. My hands shook and I shivered madly. I tried again, and this time it slipped in and turned. I thanked God briefly as another blinding jolt of loss stole my breath once more.

The thud of the door closing behind me impinged and I dropped to the floor, curling up on the thick carpet, giving into the intense sensations of pain and anguish. The flood was swift, but not terribly cleansing. At the end I felt awful, headachy, and lethargic.

"Panadol. I need panadol," I muttered into the emptiness, and was struck anew at how empty my apartment felt. It certainly wasn't a home; it was quite simply, the place I existed when I wasn't working.

I headed for the kitchen and found the painkillers before I poured a glass of water. I was alone. Today was my birthday, I realized, and I was here, in my apartment, alone. In the cold brutal light of day, I had to question my reactions.

Had I over-reacted? I had to accept that, yes, maybe I had.

"Oh no!" I sat with a thump on the small barstool, looking sightlessly into the street. Saturday morning shoppers hurried by my window, heading for streets and cafes further afield. Many with their arms slung through others chatting and laughing. But I was here, on my own. And now I was bitterly regretting the words and torrent of anger that had escaped. The scathing attack on Johnathon had been tremendously over the top.

Because I had tagged him with all the sins of my last boyfriend, Simon, back in Australia. Simon had taken my heart and trampled it with his infidelity. He was the one who had a girl-in- every-port attitude toward commitment. I remembered the look on his face and the way he'd responded to my demand that I be the only girl he slept with. His 'Sweetheart, it doesn't mean anything. It's just a way to relieve the pressure when I'm away from you.' The memory of his words had chased me halfway around the world to London.

Hindsight was a wonderful thing, I mused as the sting of pain gnawed at me once more. I'd met the perfect man and thrown away any possibility because I'd slugged him with the sins of another. Dammit, I'd only known Johnathon a handful of hours and I missed him. Without realizing it, I'd fallen into something with him. Was it love? I didn't want to admit to it, but I had known it before I left, and there it was again. The truth. There was a fair dose of lust wound up in it all. But I was no one's fool.

Could I somehow fix this? Maybe I could track him down, I thought as the memory bit deep. I could ring the hotel, see if he was still there, surely. I reached into my purse, finding the card for the hotel and went so far as to lift the receiver before the next thought assailed me. What was I going to say? Hell, I didn't even know his last name.

I dropped the receiver with nerveless fingers. I'd been stupid. Another torrent of anguish lashed me and I gave in. Sobs ripped through me as I let my head rest on the serving bar.

EVENING CAME SLOWLY. I STEPPED INTO THE SHOWER, feeling empty and spent. My lonely

meal would be something I pulled from the freezer. I didn't have the heart to cook. I refused to go out, knowing I was morose. It seemed wasteful to order in.

I stepped into the shower, the water a mere trickle as it rained down upon me. "If only it were this simple to wash away memories." I braced my arms against the tiled wall.

But there was no answer to my comment. How could there be? I was alone.

I toweled off, my body still a little sore from the marathon lovemaking I'd experienced with Johnathon. After the last couple of years of celibacy, my body was unused to sexual exercise, except with trusty old BOB, but I didn't want that now. All I wanted was Johnathon.

Memories of him touching me hammered at my mind again and I felt my body clench with desire. "Stupid girl. You never had him really. He was scratching an itch just the same way you were." But that truth didn't help me at all. I didn't feel any better for the straight talk. I sighed, throwing the towel onto the clothing basket. "I can deal with the washing later." I muttered the words, thankful for the small sound to fill the silence that had descended.

I dragged on the old velour tracksuit I'd brought from Australia with me. It was warm and comforting. My mother had chosen it for me the day after I'd announced I was leaving for England. I remembered her brave smile and the way she had told me I should follow my heart. "Ha!" I laughed, but there was no mirth. "Follow your own heart." Well, I'd done that, and look where it had gotten me.

I padded into the kitchen, pulling my hair back into a ragged ponytail. Damp strands

escaped and drips of water slipped down the back of my

top, leaving me chilled in the night air. I closed the open window with a thud.

The freezer door opened with a whoosh of cold air and I looked inside. A fettucini, an apricot chicken, and a veal chasseur sat there. I frowned, realizing how slim the choices were. "Just pick one."

My hand closed around the chicken then I shoved it back, grabbing the veal. Not exactly the haute cuisine I'd been hoping for, but it made me feel closer to my French experience and the memories of Johnathon. I threw it in the microwave, watching as it spun on the carousel. The ding alerted me it was done and I slipped it onto a plate, reached for a knife and fork from the drawer, and retreated to the eatery.

Even as I peeled back the plastic covering I sighed. It wouldn't taste half as good as some of the food I'd eaten in France during my aborted weekend away. Tears slipped down my face again. Misery sure seemed to love my company at the moment. I was sick of my own company, but didn't know how to dig myself out of the mire I had descended into.

I ate slowly, the taste was thin, the dinner cool in the center, and I wondered why I even bothered with frozen dinners. I used to like cooking, and I realized I hadn't cooked in so long. Maybe that was it? Maybe it was time to re-evaluate my lifestyle.

"It won't fix everything." I heard my words and agreed with myself. It sure wouldn't fix everything, but it was a step in what I thought could be the right direction.

I squared my shoulders, finished the last of my unsatisfying dinner, and sat there, formulating a way forward. Should I make a list and go shopping tomorrow? That might be a reasonable place to start. I stood, pushing back the barstool and hearing it scrape over the tiles.

Paper and pen were required. Not only was I going to make a grocery list, I planned to write down what I felt I needed to achieve in the next little while. The time had come to take some action. After all, wallowing was never my style, and if I continued like this, I was going to have serious problems with my own company.

My small office space was the second bedroom, so I headed in that direction, knowing there would be notepads and pens waiting. As I reached the door, someone rang my doorbell.

"Who would be calling at this time of night?"

I shrugged; it was probably someone looking for my neighbor. He was a popular rising soap star and it wasn't uncommon for people to be searching for him.

With a deep breath, I made my way to the front door, flicking on the light as the bell rang again. "I'm coming. Hold onto your knickers!"

The handle squeaked under my touch and I pulled the door open, ready to launch into a diatribe. It went unspoken though, because there stood a man with sandy blond hair and gray eyes. Johnathon.

He swept me into his arms. "Do you know how hard you are to track down?"

My head whirled. Johnathon had his arms around me and was here. Not some figment of my imagination.

"How did you find me?"

He grimaced and reached into his pocket, pulling out a dog-eared business card. It didn't have my home address, but it did have my name.

"We need to talk." The words no girl ever wanted to

hear, except in this instance. It couldn't be all that bad, could it? After all, he'd come looking for me.

"Then you'd better come in," I said. He brushed past me and I cast a quick glance outside. There were a couple of cars pulled up at the curb, idling. "Umm, are they yours?"

He looked around with a sigh. "Yeah."

"Oh. Do they want to..."

He smiled and shook his head. "No, they're quite comfortable out there at the moment." I nodded, but still felt a little uncomfortable and shut the door. He wandered into the lounge and waited.

"Sit down." I indicated a seat and he looked at me.

"Not until you do."

Oh great, now he turns gentlemanly on me. I controlled the snicker that rose. "I'm going to grab a coffee. Do you want one?"

"That'd be great." He smiled and followed me to my small galley kitchen. He liked his coffee white and with no sugar, like me. I set about making the drinks. The silence remained unbroken, but unlike earlier in the day, this was warm. It filled me with a budding emotion that made me feel complete and whole.

I replaced the container of milk in the fridge and turned to him. "Okay, so how the hell
did you find me?"

He grinned. "Well, we really need to go back to who I am, I guess."

I looked at him, seeing utter embarrassment and a tinge of pink creep over his cheeks. "We can sit down first if it helps."

He nodded and I had the distinct impression he thought that I might not like his answers. "So?" I prompted him once we were back in the lounge. He looked across the room at me

while I waited.

"It's... I'm..." He stopped and started, took a sip of his coffee then placed the mug on the small coffee table beside his chair.

I waited. I wasn't going to give him a get-out-of-jail pass this time. He needed to tell me and I needed to hear.

"You're right. I did lie. But it was a lie of omission. I should have told you about my minders. Because of who I am, I need them. My older sister was abducted seven years ago and held for ransom. Another attempt was made on my younger sister. So it's something we've had to learn to live with."

That sort of lifestyle seemed cloying to my mind. But there was more to the story, so I waited a little longer.

"My father is the founder of Horncrofts Banking."

I sucked in a deep breath. Horncrofts Banking and Financial Services was one of the biggest worldwide. It was also the financial services business that employed me straight out of college and transferred me to London after the Simon episode. That made him...

"You're my boss?"

He winced. "Not exactly. Well, not yet. See, this was supposed to be the last holiday I took before moving into the executive services branch. My father wants to retire in a year or two, and I needed to have experience before taking over from him. In the last few years, I've been working in the subsidiaries in the US and Canada. I only got home three weeks ago and have been acclimating to being home before returning to work."

The boss's son. I've been having wild monkey sex with

the boss's son and didn't even know it. It felt wrong on so many levels.

"So... Ahh, how did you track me down then?"

This time he didn't just blush, he also turned away, but not before I caught the sight of shame of his face. "I used the online systems to get your details. It took me all damned day, because I had to get my PA to track down all the necessary permissions."

Hell, he'd done that to track me down after what I'd said to him?

"But I... I treated you so badly. I yelled at you. I told you not to come looking for me." The strangled words escaped and he looked back into my face.

"I couldn't let you go, not that easily. I don't know why. I knew that if I did then my future would be lacking something really important."

I couldn't break the connection of our shared gaze.

"You were really upset. Even if you didn't want to talk to me again, I needed to make sure you got home safely. I felt like I at least owed that to you."

"I was upset." I nodded and determined that maybe I should explain everything too, so the air between us was clear. "I overreacted because in the past—"

He leaned forward, mouth open ready to interject. I raised a hand, signaling I needed to finish explaining.

"I'd been with this guy. He had all these girlfriends. I thought I was it until I caught sight of a photo of him and another girl kissing. He told me I was his girl and the others satisfied these urges. I haven't been too trusting of men since then."

He scowled and reached out a hand.

I took it, accepting his support, with a gulp and continued slowly. "That's the real reason I accepted the transfer to London. I needed to get away and build a new life. I did that, but it's empty. Lonely."

He stood and gently helped me to rise. "It doesn't have to be lonely anymore."

My breath stopped and so did my heart. What is he offering me? I hardly dared to hope or even question his words. "What? What exactly do you mean?"

He gave a nervous laugh. "I know we are only new together, but I'd like to see where this can take us. With you, I feel better, stronger, and free. Like the world is full of promise and passion. I'm not exactly the world's most eloquent man, but I get the distinct impression the sun shines brighter and there is hope in the world when I'm around you."

"I'd really like that too." Being flustered left me feeling warm and unsure, but I needed to make sure he knew I felt the same. That I wanted the same things he did. "I mean, I want to find out what the future holds too. Being without you hurt. It left me feeling like I'd left more than just a tiny piece of myself in Paris with you. And I didn't like it. I spent the entire day in a puddle, regretting those words. I shouldn't have ever said them."

He placed gentle fingers under my chin and lifted it. "Never be sorry. Without that being said, I don't know that I would have woken up to how badly I had gone about getting you into my bed and keeping you there."

Then his gaze dipped to my lips and he leaned in.

As he kissed me, the zing of connection skittered wildly. It zipped through my system leaving me hungry. And not for food.

"Come to bed with me," I whispered against his lips, but he raised his head and then shook it.

"No. That's where we went wrong last time."

I stared at him, amazed. "No. That wasn't where we went wrong. It was not telling each other everything from the beginning. So let's start again. Fresh." I stepped back even though my body was alive with need. "Hi, my name is Davina, and I am looking for a weekend of passion and adventure." Then I winked and he barked with laughter.

"Hello, my name is Johnathon Horncroft, and I'm pleased to make your acquaintance." Our hands touched and sparks of lightning must surely have flicked between them, because heaven knows the curl of heat grew in my belly.

"So let's go get naked and horizontal!"

This time he laughed out loud before sobering up. "I'd love to, but with my people outside..." He nodded toward the door and I felt ashamed that I'd forgotten his bodyguards.

"Oh. Oh dear, what's best?" My voice trailed away.

"You could come back to my place. Then it's no longer a problem."

I gulped and weighed the offer. I still had one day left of my long weekend. I could spend

it here alone, wishing I was with Johnathon, or rolling around on what I guessed would be a mighty fine, damned big bed with him. My decision was made. "Can I grab my suitcase? I haven't unpacked yet."

He grinned. "Show me where it is and I'll get it for you."

Within minutes we were in his very comfortable car, speeding toward his house, hands twined together. I'd felt a little on the spot when his driver opened the door, but Johnathon whispered a particularly wicked idea in my ear and that had left me feeling hot all over again. No doubt exactly as he had hoped.

I paid no attention to the road. Instead, I focused on how right it felt to be together and how much I wanted this man beside me. By the time we entered his very large house, my pussy was clenched and damp, my nipples hard beads of frustrated passion.

He hustled me up a long corridor and shoved open a door. Before the door shut, his mouth was scorching mine, his tongue down my throat, and his hands in my panties, searching for my core. My own hands were doing a similar job on him, wrenching at the buckle of his belt, tearing at his fine linen shirt while the studs clicked and released.

He lifted his head and mine whirled. "I need you inside me. I need you to fill me up and make me scream."

We stilled, watching each other in the semi darkness of the bedroom. "I don't want to use a rubber with you. I want to feel your heat. I want whatever might come."

It took me a minute until I understood what he was saying, that we see where nature took this thing between us. If a child were a natural outcome then we would both welcome it. I smiled. "That sounds good to me. So long as this is going to be a relationship."

He grinned. "I sure as hell hope so." Then he stripped off his jacket, shirt, and pants. He stopped, looking a little lost for a second.

"I haven't ever done it without one before either."

He grinned and that was all that was needed to close the discussion.

My hands moved to my own clothes, shucking them slowly, while my body readied itself for him and his sensual invasion. We finally stood naked and he leaned in, licking the distended tip of one breast.

"Have I told you how much I love your breasts? They are just right." He sucked one into his mouth and I moaned, my legs moving slightly as his fingers combed their way through the damp hairs. He slipped two fingers deep within my ready sheath, moving them slowly, and my legs sagged.

"Not that way. Not this time. Please?"

He released me, and I sought the support of the wall, but he wasn't done with me yet. He slipped his arms beneath my legs, raised me up, and carried me over to his bed before gently laying me upon the quilt.

I shifted, making room for him, and he crawled between my legs. "Then I shall fill you up, my lady." He fitted himself at the entrance to my core and slowly eased his hard length inside. Each move grabbing the last bit of sanity I possessed.

He rocked once and stopped. It was enough to have me arching in his steely embrace. Then he moved again and I undulated with him, needing to participate in this ancient dance. Faster, we worked against each other, needing more and more of the touches and sighs.

Finally I splintered, screaming his name, and he pumped me harder and faster. Pushing himself deeply within me before he too climaxed. I felt the pulsing sensation of jetting seed. Something I hadn't experienced before him. It felt right on every level.

We lay still, wrapped in each other's arms. "I won't make you any promises yet. I nearly lost you because of what I didn't say and held back. The only one I can and will make is that I will be honest with you."

I smiled. "I know." I drowsed in his arms, watching as day followed night in the large window in front of the bed. It was a new year for me. And it was filled with promise.

EPILOGUE

Paris in the summer was probably one of my favorite places and times. It reminded me of last year.

This time last year, I'd been here on my own, sitting in this same bar, drinking wine. This year, here I was in the same place at the same time. I watched as the clock struck three AM and laughed. "This time last year you were about to explode into my life."

Johnathon smiled at me. "I have a present for you."

"Oh now, come on. This holiday is enough..."

He stilled my words with the shake of a head. "No. I need to do this." He looked at me.

"Sit still. Don't say anything until I ask, okay?"

"Okay." I waited quietly, nursing my drink as he stood and wandered toward the door. He spoke quietly to the French woman I now knew to be a distant cousin and security

specialist. She spoke quickly, and while my French had definitely improved during my time with Johnathon, it wasn't enough to understand their conversation. She grinned and handed him a packet tied up with a silver and hot pink bow before glancing at me and winking.

I was getting better at having people around me, knowing my business, but it still felt odd at times like this. To cover my discomfort, I took a sip of the soda water, tasting the tangy flavor. Then he stood in front of me. I started to rise, but he laid a hand on my shoulder. "Stay where you are."

His words perplexed me, but I waited as he cleared his throat and looked around. Suddenly no one was facing our direction. What the—

He dropped to one knee and I nearly swallowed my tongue. "Davina Chandler. I've lived with you full time for six months, known you for twelve, and loved you for all of it. Marry me and make me the happiest man alive?"

His gaze was hopeful and I knew I couldn't leave him waiting. This man I loved more than life had been generous, kind, understanding, and most importantly loving. He'd survived my bad days, celebrated my good ones, and even stayed by my side during my monthly PMS sessions. "How can I not? I have loved you since the first moment, I think. Even when I flew home last year, I knew I couldn't ever be apart from you."

He whooped, surged to his feet, and handed me the gaily wrapped packet. "Open it. If you don't like it, I'll have something else made up for you."

My fingers trembled as I undid the bow, and there nestled within was a ring box. I was too scared to open it and thrust it back into his hands. "Please. You do it."

He smiled and flipped open the box. On a bed of white satin lay the most exquisite emerald ring I'd ever seen.

It winked under the lights and I extended my hand. "Please?"

As he slipped it onto my finger, I knew it was a promise. Just like the other one. The envelope in my pocket all but screamed at me to hand it over, so I fumbled a little and placed it in his hands. "Here's a present for you."

He frowned and opened the packet. A grainy picture caught his eyes then he looked into mine. "Yours? Ours?"

I nodded and placed my palm against his cheek. "In another six and a half months."

His gaze dropped to my waist. "We'd better get cracking then. Next year, when we come back here there'll be three of us."

"Yes, there will. Maybe we should come back each year to celebrate how important Paris is to us."

"You'd better count on it."

And I did, because I knew his words were a vow.

INHERITANCE OF THE BLOOD BY IMOGENE NIX

In the darkness evil waits…

As a young bride Kira was whisked away from everything and everyone she knew, including her new husband and became Christina, an operative of the Displaced Persons Unit.

As the danger grows she sees an opportunity to save her husband Vasya and sister Serina. But nothing is the same. Serina is grown up—married and pregnant.

Vasya too is older and darkly forbidding. Trusting Christina doesn't come easily until a catastrophic event takes place. Now, knowing the truth everything he thought he knew is changed. But at a very high cost.

The four must work together to defeat the Demon, Zuor and the stakes are higher than they imagined and all could be lost.

The burning at the back of her neck warned she was being watched. A quick glance didn't clarify it. Instead, she turned around in time to see her mother's face, pale. "Mama?"

She took a step forward, but her grandfather snatched her wrist.

The grip was painful, and Kira stilled. "Let your parents talk."

She didn't know what the topic of conversation was, but it couldn't be good.

The dappled sunlight seemed cooler than before.

Her father crooked his forefinger at her grandfather while they stood there. For a moment she wished Vasya had come with them, but he had to work. Just the thought of her new husband warmed Kira.

She only had a few minutes to contemplate her newly defined status as a married woman, when her grandfather pulled at her hand. "Come with me." He tugged and, confused, Kira allowed herself to be towed away.

A glance at her parents' faces stole any feeling of well-being.

"Grandfather?"

"Shh, my love. You must go." His grip was implacable and his face stern, but he shivered.

"What are you doing? Where are you taking me, Grandfather?"

They moved rapidly through the village they'd visited to sell their wares just that morning, and for the first time since they'd arrived in the market place she felt fear. What was wrong? Was it something to do with Vasya?

"You are in danger. We must send you away." The words confused her further. Send her away? Danger?

"Where is Vasya?" She stumbled over a stone, but he kept tugging her onwards.

With a quick glance around, he hauled her into a dirty laneway between the buildings. Kira gasped, trying to drag air into her starving lungs. "There's no time. We must get you away."

A nondescript shopfront lay ahead, and he pushed on the door. It rattled and opened with a loud groan. "Andre? Andre, are you here?"

An older man shuffled into the room, bent nearly double from the weight of the load on his back. "Marat? What do you want?"

"My granddaughter. They are coming for her and us. Get her away. Take her now, while you can."

The man's face clouded over. "Are you sure?"

"Grandfather, where is Vasya?" Fright had the blood in her veins pounding.

"Hush, my precious. Andre will see you well." He turned. "Whatever it takes, Andre. Take her now." With surprising speed, her grandfather whirled and was gone.

The man, Andre, eyed her. "Come this way, child. There is no time to be lost."

Eleven years later

The tattoo of her heart and cry of terror woke her, as they usually did. Once again, as she had since that rapid flight from those who sought her, she found herself in a lonely bed. Hundreds of miles away from everything she'd dreamed of, in a house she'd built for them to share. As always, it left her wishing that Vasya had fled with her.

Instead, here she was, exiled without her husband. With a sob, she rolled over and let the tears fall.

Available from Beachwalk Press
books2read.com/IOTB

Direct Autographed Copy
http://bit.ly/2w6g4K6

When Cupid—otherwise known as Diocail— is banished from his home on a remote Scottish Island, he's set a series of tasks by the great god Lugh, who also happens to be his father.

In **Blame The Wine**, he must bring two lovers together... BBW Cara and James, the man she's lusted over from afar who happens to be a super geek and head Veha Industries.

In **A Stranger's Embrace**, Diocail is driven to help

an emotionally fragile Jane and Davis, a famous author. The task is more complicated, with the existence of Carstairs her could-be ex-husband and teenage daughter, Frannie.

In **_Revenge on Cupid_**, Diocail must take the ultimate chance and find his own happily ever after with Simone. Sometimes the past gets in the way and HEA's don't come cheap though.

The dusty, dingy little diner was full, even with its current state of cleanliness—or lack thereof. People from the surrounding offices didn't care about anything except the incredible, well-prepared food at a reasonable cost. They flooded in, like waves to the shore. As one tide left, another swept in.

"Honestly, Simone. I'm going to try getting his attention one more time. If that doesn't work, I'm out of there. I mean, how long can I keep trying?" Cara picked at the caramel tart she hadn't been able to resist with the cheap metal fork and flicked the blob of fresh cream that sat on top to the side of the plate.

"You've said that tons of times before. Besides, what are you going to do to get his attention? Hmm? Walk naked through the typing pool?" Simone bobbed the straw in her smoothie as she eyed her friend with a frown. "It's been what? Eighteen months since you saw him, and you've mooned over him from a distance ever since you met him. You need to move on, Cara. That is, unless there's something you haven't shared?"

The query was arch. Cara shivered even as she shook her head. "No."

Simone quirked an eyebrow, obviously unconvinced with the answer. Cara let out a deep sigh of frustration. "There's a position...it's only temporary, for a PA reporting directly to him." She speared a forkful of tart, chewed quickly and swallowed, before continuing. "In his office, full-time for the period of the engagement. I saw the memo yesterday. I mean, I have the skills, right? I can type, answer phones, make coffee, file, greet people. What's more, I can probably do it better than all those size eights in the typing pool that Ms. Jackman seems to prefer." She nodded thoughtfully. "All I have to do is get past the ogre in Human Resources."

Simone stared at her, disbelief clear on her face. "Girl, I so remember that woman. If you think you can get past her, you're doing better than I ever did. That's why I left Veha Industries, remember? Maybe it's time to haul out your resumé and consider some other options. Look for something better." Simone shook her head and billows of her crimson hair swirled through the still air.

Cara understood Simone only had her best interests at heart. But this time she knew the outcome would be different. Hell, she could feel it in the air. The tingle of expectation.

"Cara, the HR ogre will hang you out for breakfast before she offers you anything like a position in that office. Remember her mantra? Good looks and good work make for a positive workplace!"

Simone didn't sugar-coat anything. It was another great reason for their long- term friendship. Honesty. But Cara didn't want to hear the truth in the statement. Even if it was exactly as her friend said.

Cara nodded quickly. "Yeah, I know, but if I don't try, then I won't know how close I can get to him, right? And the only way to catch his attention is to get past *her* and see him in person." Cara quaked a little at the information she needed to share. The favor she needed to ask. "Anyway, I tidied up my resumé and dropped the application into a memo envelope yesterday, so it's too late to back out now. I mean, fortune favors the brave. Doesn't it? If I don't snag an interview, I'm going to visit the career advisor across the street and register with them." She shrugged. "I'll look for temp work until something more long-term shows up. I can see what they have on offer and well...who knows? Maybe a job with the right boss is just waiting for me. But I'd rather this worked out, to be honest." Her voice trailed off into a whisper. "I really wish he would notice me."

Simone took a long slurp of her banana drink, and Cara noticed her questioning gaze even as she squirmed. Finally, Simone nodded. "It's your funeral. So anyway, you'd better show me this memo if you want me to be a referee for you. I'm guessing that's what you need, right? I'll have to know what I'm supposed to say about you before they ring."

Cara smiled. "Thanks, Simone. I knew I could count on you." She slipped a piece of paper out of her handbag and handed it over. "Sorry it's a bit creased. It was in the bottom of my bag, I stashed it so none of the others from the pool would see. You know how it is."

Available from Love Books Publishing
books2read.com/CelticCupid

Direct Autographed Copy
http://bit.ly/2vs7wtS

BIOCYBE BY IMOGENE NIX

Can a cyber-enhanced warrior and a ship's captain find love together?

Levia Endrado never wanted to be a warrior, but at seventeen she was deemed suitable for battle. After intense training and multiple enhancements, which gave her superior strength and healing ability, she was sent off to defeat the enemy—a killing machine with a mission.

When the war was over, she had to find a new life. At twenty-seven she's a washed-up veteran without a future. Or she was, until she met Sandon Daria.

Serving as a pilot aboard Sandon's spaceship the *Golden Echo* makes Levia long for a different and gentler life. But old hurts and even older enemies aren't so easily forgotten. Particularly when they come back for her.

Sandon is determined to show Levia that she's more than just a BioCybe...she's the woman who completes him. Getting close is just the first step, keeping her alive is an even bigger challenge, but one he's willing to take because the prize is their combined future.

Levia scanned the long line of other hopefuls entering the chamber. The large building in the center of town was cold, and she dragged her wrap around her body, even as she craned her head, looking to the high ceiling. She'd never before had an occasion to enter the testing complex, yet she'd seen the lines of teenagers every time they passed the building.

Once she'd asked her parents why the teens were lined up and her mother's face had shuttered. Her stepfather had just shaken his head and growled. They'd stopped her questions with a carefully uttered, "You'll know soon enough, Levia." The pain in her mother's eyes had been enough to shush her questions. For endless months afterward, her parents had traveled different routes to the educational facility she attended and Levia lost interest in the puzzle of that building.

Now, as she looked around, remembering that long ago spring day, it was her opportunity to find out. But she felt a surge of concern at what lay ahead. She likely wasn't the only one, given that there were probably two to three hundred seventeen-year-olds gathered in the one place. Ahead of her, she caught sight of a couple of girls, their arms linked together and wide smiles on their faces. Scanning the crowd, she became aware that, by far, a majority of those gathered displayed both fear and trepidation.

"All female subjects will enter through doors three, six, and seven. All male subjects will enter through gates four, eight, and ten." The speaker above her was loud, and she jumped before checking the numbers etched on the black metal sign over her head.

The massive doors beside her swung open, and now an uncertain silence reigned. Many of the youngsters hung back, clearly discomforted by whatever testing regime lay ahead. This was where they'd been told their futures would be determined.

"Oh gosh, I hope they only have an aptitude and psych eval. I don't think..." Levia turned to see the white face of the girl behind her. The girl had uttered what many must silently be thinking.

Levia dragged an unsteady breath in, her hand resting flat against the plane of her belly as she looked around. No one had entered yet. It was clear many were on the verge of taking the step, but still they hung back.

She straightened her shoulders. "I'm not afraid." It was always wiser to approach things head-on, she believed. When her biological father had died, she'd been one of the few to view his capsule before it was sent into the massive gray structure built to accommodate those who'd moved onto the next life realm.

Her legs shook as she wobbled toward the entrance. Beyond the doorway, she spied sealed cubicles and her heart stuttered. Why cubicles? Usually testing—med and psych—were in eval-units, hidden only by billowing white curtains. She glanced back, noting that others had taken the first step.

"Move along, subjects." Once again, the androgynous voice of the address system blared.

Of course, given it was her seventeenth anniversary of birth, she was technically considered an adult now.

She thought longingly of baby Rald and her half-sister, Elda, waiting at home for her to return, and the celebrations to be held that night. That made her smile. She would need to make them proud of her.

She entered a row and the tall Educational Specialist, the edu-specs as her peers laughingly called them, stopped her. "Present your credentials to the scanner."

She'd done this many times since the tiny implant had been slipped below the dermal layer of her skin at birth. The small unit in her wrist heated as her details were checked.

"Enter the first cubicle, Levia Endrado, and follow the instructions to complete your assessment."

Thus dismissed, Levia moved to the first unit, laid her palm against the scanner, and the door slid open soundlessly.

"Welcome, Levia Endrado. Take your place in the eval-unit." The soft contralto of the voice echoed after the door closed silently behind her.

"What are you evaluating?" Her voice was breathy, and she peered around.

"Your   skills—physical   and   psychological.   Your

emotional and medical status. Your educational attainment levels."

It was an answer that shed little insight into the many things she was hungry to know. "Why do all seventeen year olds—"

"Take a seat, Levia. Then we may begin your testing."

If she'd expected an answer, she was sadly mistaken, she considered sourly. She dropped into the seat, the soft leather-like surface molding to her body.

"Levia Endrado, you are required to remove all non-specified apparel."

She jolted in the chair. "It's cold."

"The temperature will be amended. Remove the non-specified apparel."

Her misgivings grew as she dragged off the light wrap she'd brought with her, and then threw it to the floor at the side of the unit.

"We will begin, Levia Endrado. At any time, should you experience any malfunctions of the unit, simply depress the red button." It glowed and she grimaced.

Levia reclined against the chair and waited for the testing to begin.

The first examination was based on her understanding of the political system, where she saw herself, and her knowledge of the rights and responsibilities accorded through citizenship of both her planet and the commonwealth.

The second test was mathematical and scientific proficiency. It felt like hours had passed by the time she'd finished, and she lay limp on the seat, exhausted.

"Levia Endrado, you may rise. The sanitary unit will emerge once you trigger the yellow button at the door.

Should you require refreshment, press the blue button and a restorative will be made available."

"Can I leave?"

"Negative, Levia Endrado. Your needs will be catered for in this capsule."

"Why?" Her voice hitched and true fear rose for the first time. Why did they keep her in the alcove?

"All will be revealed at the end of the testing cycle."

Levia looked at the now empty screen before hurling a curse word. It was met with silence.

The urgent throb of her bladder reminded her that she needed to use the facilities, so, with

a sigh, she rose and clambered from the seat. After attending to the needs of her body, she walked around the unit, peering at the door, but it was obviously programmed remotely. She poked and prodded, but it made no difference. With a huff, she headed back to the chair.

The moment she'd settled in, the viewing screen shone bright. "Welcome back, Levia. The next sequence will evaluate your psychological reflexes, then that will be followed up with the general knowledge portion of the evaluation."

"When can I leave?" It seemed better to ask bluntly, she told herself.

"Once the examination is completed. After the next set of evaluations, you will be subjected to the physical aspect."

"Then I can go home?"

"Levia Endrado, you will now complete the psychological test. This will be undertaken by one of the center's personal evaluators."

She frowned. Personal evaluators? She bit her lip, and the sting reminded her that this wasn't something to joke about. In her seventeen years, she'd only heard of personal evaluators being brought in once before, and that was when one of the girls at her academy had been in a serious accident. Both legs were amputated and her body's ability to keep her alive had been gravely compromised. Her peers had been informed that the girl had requested the assessment before she could request her support systems be disconnected.

"Levia Endrado, are you ready to recommence processing?" The emotionless voice echoed once more and she gulped.

"Yes."

Available from Beachwalk Press
http://www.beachwalkpress.com

Direct Autographed Books
http://bit.ly/BioCybe

- Executing Justice

The Reunion Trilogy in Paperback

Sex Love & Aliens

- Tangled Webs
- False Webs
- Covert Webs

21st Testing Protocol

- Cyborg: Redux
- Children Of A Greater Evil (Not Yet Released)
- When Evil Came To Stay (Not Yet Released)
- Finis: The War To End All Wars (Not Yet Released)

Celtic Cupid Trilogy

- Blame The Wine
- A Stranger's Embrace
- Revenge On Cupid

The Celtic Cupid Trilogy in Paperback (August 2019)

Zombieology

- The Reset (2018)
- I Dream of Zombies (2019)
- The Six Million Dollar Zombie (Not Yet Released)

Knights of Pleasure

- Silken Knights (Not Yet Released)

<u>Single Titles</u>

The Chocolate Affair

Falling In Love Again (Previously A Sapphire For Karina)

BioCybe

Hesparia's Tears

Tomorrow's Promise

A Bar In Paris (also coming to paperback)

Inheritance Of The Blood

The Plan

Loving Memories (also coming to paperback)

Hero of Heartbreak Hill

Raspberry Dreams (Not Yet Released)

<u>Non Fiction</u>

Self Publishing: Absolute Beginners Guide (With Suzi Love)

<u>Written as Ciara Cave</u>

25 Curated Ways To Get Rid Of Telemarketers

Book Signings for Absolute Beginners

ABOUT THE AUTHOR

Imogene is published in a range of romance genres including Paranormal, Science Fiction and Contemporary. She is mainly published in the UK and USA.

In 2010, Imogene Nix (the pen name not Imogene herself) was born. Imogene sat down and worked tirelessly for 3 months culminating in the book Starline, which became the first in a trilogy titled, "Warriors of the Elector." Since then she's had over 30 titles published and is now focusing on hybridising herself - with a mixture of traditionally published and self-published works.

In fact, she's taking control of many of her back catalogue books, which are slowly re-releasing as self-published titles.

Imogene is a member of a range of professional organisations world wide, and believes in the mantra of mentoring and paying it forward and is actively involved in mentorship (through NaNoWrimo and her vlog: In The Chair With Imogene Nix) and tutoring of new and upcoming authors.

In her spare time she loves to drink coffee, wine & eat chocolate and is parenting her spoiled dog and a ferocious cat along with her husband and 2 human daughters and looks forward to weekends away with her husband in their caravan "The Seven Year Hitch!" Do look forward to her caravan romance at some point!

To Contact Imogene
www.imogenenix.net
imogene@imogenenix.net

facebook.com/ImogeneNix

twitter.com/ImogeneNix

instagram.com/ImogeneNix